新雅兒童英文圖解字典

慣用語
Idioms

Elaine Tin　著

in hot water
陷入麻煩

on the way to
即將完成

新雅文化事業有限公司
www.sunya.com.hk

如何使用新雅點讀筆閱讀本書?

新雅・點讀樂園 **升級**功能

讓孩子學習更輕鬆愉快!

　　本系列屬「新雅點讀樂園」產品之一,若配備新雅點讀筆,孩子可以點讀書中的字詞和相關例句的內容,聆聽英語和粵語,或是英語和普通話的發音。

　　想了解更多「新雅點讀樂園」產品,請瀏覽新雅網頁(www.sunya.com.hk)或掃描右邊的QR code進入 新雅・點讀樂園 。

Sun
太陽

1. 下載本書的點讀筆檔案

1 瀏覽新雅網頁(www.sunya.com.hk) 或掃描右邊的 QR code 進入 新雅•點讀樂園 。

2 點選 下載點讀筆檔案 ▶ 。

3 依照下載區的步驟說明,點選及下載《新雅兒童英文圖解字典》的點讀筆檔案至電腦,並複製至新雅點讀筆的「BOOKS」資料夾內。

2. 啟動點讀功能

開啟點讀筆後,請點選封面右上角的 新雅•點讀樂園 圖示,然後便可翻開書本,點選書本上字詞、圖畫或句子,點讀筆便會播放相應的內容。

3. 選擇語言

如想切換播放語言,請點選內頁右上角的圖示,當再次點選內頁時,點讀筆便會使用所選的語言播放點選的內容。

如何使用本字典？

《新雅兒童英文圖解字典：慣用語》適合幼稚園至初小學生，收錄超過360個慣用語。每個詞目均附中文釋義、漢語拼音、雙語例句，並配以精美插圖，內容清楚，一目了然。

全書把慣用語分為12個主題，包括身體、顏色、動物、自然、交通、時間、說話、飲食、物件、動作、否定，以及其他。

中文釋義上方提供漢語拼音，幫助孩子學習中文字詞的漢語發音。

身體　ENG×粵語　ENG×普通話

make sb's mouth water

令人垂涎欲滴
lìng rén chuí xián yù dī

38

例句

The chocolate fountain makes my mouth water.

這個朱古力噴泉令我垂涎欲滴。

chocolate的普通話是「巧克力」。

利用新雅點讀筆點選圖示，可切換播放語言。

為方便閱讀，詞目中的 somebody 簡化為 sb 或 one；something 簡化為 sth。

英文例句示範詞目的正確用法，中文翻譯方便讀者掌握意思。

鑑於粵普用字略有不同，為便利孩子學習，本書會按需提供粵普詞彙對照。

本書為入門級的慣用語字典，旨在幫助學童掌握詞目的基本釋義，學習地道英語。在內容編排上，本書精選幼稚園至初小程度必學的慣用語，一個單頁呈現一個詞目，幫助孩子輕鬆學習，培養英文語感。

部分慣用語多用於某些特定情境，故此本字典會按需提供相關文字說明。

有些慣用語在不同英語地區會有不同用字，此字框會按需收載其他常見說法，讓孩子多吸收地道英語，提升英文水平。

本字典部分例句為對話形式，以便學童掌握慣用語的具體使用情境。

目錄

✦ 顏色

✦ 動物

✦ 自然

✦ 交通

✦ 時間

✦ 說話

✦ 飲食

✦ 物件

✦ 動作

✦ 否定

✨ 其他

a shoulder to cry on

kě qīng sù de duì xiàng
可傾訴的對象

 例句

Whenever I feel sad, mum is always a shoulder to cry on.

每當我感到難過，媽媽總是我的傾訴對象。

all eyes are on sth

bèi shòu guān zhù
備受關注

 例句 -

All eyes are on the swimming final tonight.

今晚舉行的游泳決賽備受關注。

身體

ENG × 粵語　ENG × 普通話

be all ears

zhuān xīn líng tīng
專心聆聽

22

✦ 例句 --------------------------------

The tourists were all ears when the guide was explaining the history of the temple.

遊客專心聆聽導遊講解廟宇的歷史。

be all eyes

mù bù zhuǎn jīng
目不轉睛

 例句

The audience were all eyes as the clown juggled the balls.

觀眾目不轉睛地看着小丑拋雜耍球。

bear in mind

láo jì
牢記

24

✨ **例句** -

Children, bear in mind you have to return all the tools before you leave.

小朋友，記住在離開前交還所有工具。

by a nose

yǐ shāo wēi yōu shì qǔ shèng
以稍微優勢（取勝）

 例句 -

He won the race by a nose.

他以稍微優勢勝出這場比賽。

cannot believe one's eyes

bù xiāng xìn suǒ kàn jiàn de
不相信所看見的

 例句 ----------------------------

I could not believe my eyes when I saw my dog playing with a cat.

看見我的狗和貓玩耍時，我不敢相信自己的眼睛。

cost an arm and a leg

jí qí áng guì
極其昂貴

✨ **例句** --------------------------------

The sports car cost him an arm and a leg.

這輛跑車花費了他大量金錢。

cry one's eyes out

háo kū

嚎哭

 例句 -

She cried her eyes out because she had dropped her ice cream.

她嚎哭起來,因為她把雪糕丟到地上了。

ice cream的普通話是「冰淇淋」。

find one's feet

xí guàn xīn huán jìng
習慣新環境

 例句

The manager was happy to see Matthew had found his feet in his new position.

經理很高興看見馬修適應了新職位。

from the bottom of one's heart

zhōng xīn de
衷心地

30

 例句 ------------------------

She congratulated her rival from the bottom of her heart.

她衷心地祝賀對手。

give sb the cold shoulder

gù yì lěng luò
故意冷落

 例句

Even if I had apologised for being late, she still gave me the cold shoulder.

即使我已經為遲到而道歉了，但是她仍然故意冷落我。

gut feeling

zhí jué
直覺

17:45

 例句

feeling 可換成 reaction 或 instinct。

I have a gut feeling that we will not leave the office on time today.

我有種直覺,我們今天不能準時下班。

32

keep a straight face

bǎn zhe liǎn
板着臉

33

 例句

Nobody dares to talk to Mr Chan because he always keeps a straight face.

沒有人敢跟陳老師說話，因為他經常板着臉。

keep an eye on

liú shén
留神

 例句

Passengers should keep an eye on their own belongings.

乘客應該看管好自己的物品。

lend sb a helping hand

bāng zhù　　mǒu rén
幫助（某人）

✨ 例句 -

Peter, can you lend me a helping hand with the sofa?

彼得，你可以幫我一起搬沙發嗎？

lick one's lips

fēi cháng qī dài
非常期待

 例句 ----------------------------

The shoppers licked their lips when they entered the outlet mall.

顧客滿心期待地走入特賣場。

like pulling teeth

kùn nan de

困難的

 例句 ------------------------

Getting him to do homework is like pulling teeth.

要他做功課真是困難。

身體

make sb's mouth water

lìng rén chuí xián yù dī
令人垂涎欲滴

38

 例句 -

The chocolate fountain makes my mouth water.

這個朱古力噴泉令我垂涎欲滴。

chocolate的普通話是「巧克力」。

on everyone's lips

guǎng wéi tán lùn de
廣為談論的

 例句 ------------------------------

This newly released game is very popular and it is on everyone's lips.

這個新發售的遊戲很受歡迎，人人都在談論它。

身體

on its last legs

kuài yào huài le
快要壞了

 例句 -

The television screen keeps flickering.
It seems to be on its last legs.

電視機熒幕不停閃動，看來快要壞了。

身體

ENG × 粵語　ENG × 普通話

out of hand

shī kòng
失控

例句 --------------------------------

He spends too much time on his tablet and lets himself out of hand.

他花太多時間在平板電腦上,不懂自制。

play it by ear

kàn qíng kuàng ér dìng
看情況而定

 例句 -

I have no plans for this weekend. I will just play it by ear.

我沒有計劃這個周末要做什麼，會看情況而定。

身體

scream one's head off

jiān jiào
尖叫

43

例句 ----

We screamed our heads off when the light suddenly went off.

燈光突然熄滅時，我們尖叫起來。

send a chill down sb's spine

lìng rén máo gǔ sǒng rán
令人毛骨悚然

 例句

Watching you hold the snake sent a chill down my spine.

看着你抱着那條蛇，令我毛骨悚然。

ENG
×
粵語

ENG
×
普通話

skin and bones

jí dù shòu xuè
極度瘦削

例句 ------------------------

She is just skin and bones. She does not look healthy.

她太瘦削了，看起來並不健康。

slip one's mind

bèi wàng jì
被忘記

46

 例句 -

Oh! I have a dictation today. It totally slipped my mind.

噢！今天要默書，我完全忘記了。

take the weight off one's legs

zuò xià xiū xi
坐下休息

 例句

legs 可換成 feet。

Ⓐ I am exhausted!
Ⓑ Come and sit. Take the weight off your legs.
甲 我筋疲力盡了！
乙 過來坐下歇歇腳吧。

tear sb's heart out

lìng rén xīn rú dāo gē
令人心如刀割

48

 例句 --------------------------------

My best friend stopped talking to me and it tore my heart out.

我的摯友不再跟我說話，令我心如刀割。

thumbs up

biǎo shì zàn shǎng
表示讚賞

 例句

The restaurant owner gave the thumbs up to the chef's new dish.

餐廳東主對主廚的新菜色表示讚賞。

turn a deaf ear

chōng ěr bù wén
充耳不聞

  例句 -

The waiter turned a deaf ear to the customer's request.

侍應生對顧客的要求充耳不聞。

twist sb's arm

shuō fú mǒu rén
說服（某人）

 例句 ----------------------------

She did not want to come to the party but I twisted her arm.

她原本不想參加派對，但是我說服她來了。

with all one's heart

quán xīn quán yì
全心全意

52

 例句 ----------------------------

She loves dancing with all her heart.
She wants to be a ballerina.

她全心全意熱愛跳舞，想要成為芭蕾舞蹈員。

a riot of colour

sè cǎi bīn fēn
色彩繽紛

 例句 -

In spring, flowers bloom beautifully and the park is a riot of colour.

春天，鮮花盛開，公園色彩繽紛。

(as) white as a sheet

liǎn sè cāng bái
臉色蒼白

✦ 例句 --------------------------------

Are you okay? You look white as a sheet.

你沒事嗎？你看起來臉色蒼白。

black and blue

yū qīng de
瘀青的

 例句 ---------------------------

He fell off the bike so his legs were black and blue.

他從單車摔下來，雙腳都瘀青了。

✎ bike的普通話是「自行車」。

blue in the face

tú láo wú gōng
徒勞無功

 例句 -

I had asked him to clean the room until I was blue in the face, but he did not do it.

任憑我如何叫他打掃房間也沒用，他還是不去做。

born with a silver spoon in one's mouth

shēng yú fù yù jiā tíng
生於富裕家庭

 例句 -

Dave was born with a silver spoon in his mouth. He was given a house at the age of 18.

戴夫生於富裕家庭，在18歲時獲贈一所房子。

顏色

 ENG × 粵語　ENG × 普通話

catch sb red-handed

dāng chǎng zhuā zhù huài rén
當場抓住壞人

 例句 --------------------------------

The man was caught red-handed littering.

男士亂拋垃圾，被當場抓住了。

顏色

 ENG × 粵語

 ENG × 普通話

every cloud has a silver lining

hēi àn zhōng zǒng yǒu shǔ guāng
黑暗中總有曙光

 例句 -

Every cloud has a silver lining. You will get a job soon.

黑暗中總有曙光，你很快會找到工作。

 59

golden opportunity

qiān zǎi nán féng de jī huì
千載難逢的機會

✦ 例句 ------------------------------

This magic contest may be a golden opportunity for you.

這個魔術比賽可能是你千載難逢的機會。

60

green with envy

shí fēn dù jì
十分妒忌

 例句 -

The stepsisters were green with envy when Cinderella was dancing with the prince.

灰姑娘和王子跳舞時，繼姊姊們都十分妒忌。

61

grey area

huī sè dì dài
灰色地帶

 例句

> grey area 多指不清晰的規則或指引。

I thought I could come with my parrot.
There is a grey area in this sign.

我以為可以帶鸚鵡來。這個告示有灰色地帶。

have a green finger

jīng yú yuán yì
精於園藝

 例句 -

Grandpa has a green finger. He spends a lot of time on his backyard.

祖父精於園藝，他花很多時間打理後花園。

have a heart of gold

xīn dì shàn liáng
心地善良

 例句 -

She has a heart of gold — she never hesitates to help people in need.

她心地善良——她從不猶豫幫助有需要的人。

have the blues

gǎn dào yōu shāng
感到憂傷

 例句 ------------------------------

I have had the blues ever since my best friend moved to another country.

自從我的摯友移民後，我就一直感到憂傷。

in the dark

hún rán bù zhī
渾然不知

✨ 例句 -

His car has been scratched but he is in the dark.

他的車輛被刮花了，但是他渾然不知。

like gold dust

nán yǐ dé dào
難以得到

 例句 -----------------------------

This comic book is out of print. It is like gold dust.

這本漫畫書已經絕版了,珍貴難求。

out of the blue

<ruby>突<rt>tū</rt></ruby><ruby>然<rt>rán</rt></ruby>

突然

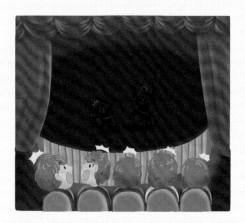

68

 例句 ----------------------------

Out of the blue, the lights on the stage went off.

舞台上的燈光突然熄滅了。

roll out the red carpet

rè liè huān yíng
熱烈歡迎

69

 例句

The crowd rolled out the red carpet for the gold medalist.

羣眾熱烈歡迎金牌運動員。

see red

fēi cháng shēng qì
非常生氣

 例句 -

Miss Wong saw red when she knew we were not paying attention in class.

黃老師知道我們上課不專心時，生氣極了。

show one's (true) colours

zhǎn xiàn zhēn xìng qíng
展現真性情

 例句 --------------------------------

Everyone thought she was shy, but she showed her colours in the party.

人人都以為她很害羞，但是她在派對上展現了自己的真性情。

顏色

the grass is always greener on the other side

bié ren de zǒng shì jiào hǎo
別人的總是較好

72

 例句

Ⓐ Her cotton candy looks bigger than mine.

Ⓑ They are the same size. The grass is always greener on the other side.

甲 她的棉花糖看起來比我的大。

乙 它們都一樣大。別人的總是較好。

ENG × 粵語
ENG × 普通話

tickled pink

fēi cháng gāo xìng
非常高興

 例句 -

Angie is tickled pink when we praise her for her drawing.

我們稱讚安琪的畫作時，安琪非常高興。

turn beet red

gān gà de liǎn hóng
尷尬得臉紅

 例句 - - - - - - - - - - - - turn 可換成 go。

When he was caught sleeping in class, he turned beet red.

他被抓到在課堂上睡覺時，尷尬得滿臉通紅。

white lie

shàn yì de huǎng yán
善意的謊言

例句 -

I told a white lie when I said her cookies were yummy.

我說了一個善意的謊言，說她的曲奇餅很好吃。

with flying colours

chū sè de
出色地

 例句

He passed the driving test with flying colours.

他通過了駕駛考試，表現出色。

yellow-bellied

dǎn xiǎo de
膽小的

例句

He is such a yellow-bellied boy. I think he will not watch this scary film.

他這麼膽小，我認為他不會看這齣恐怖電影。

a fly on the wall

àn zhōng tōu tīng zhě
暗中偷聽者

 例句 -

He always acts as a fly on the wall when the boss talks to others.

他經常偷聽老闆和別人談話。

an elephant in the room

bù yuàn tí jí de wèn tí

不願提及的問題

例句 -

Ellen is a terrible singer. It is an elephant in the room as we don't want to embarrass her.

雅倫唱歌很難聽，但是我們都不願提出來，因為不想令她尷尬。

a leopard can't change its spots

jiāng shān yì gǎi　　 běn xìng nán yí
江山易改，本性難移

例句

A leopard can't change its spots. Although he is the monitor, he is still irresponsible.

江山易改，本性難移。即使他是班長，他仍是很不負責任。

another kettle of fish

jié rán bù tóng de shì
截然不同的事

 例句 ----------------------------

I like cooking but I do not want to be a chef. It is another kettle of fish.

我喜歡烹飪，但是我不想當廚師。那完全是兩回事。

(as) blind as a bat

shì lì bù jiā
視力不佳

 例句 -

If he does not wear his glasses, he is blind as a bat.

如果他不戴眼鏡，就什麼都看不清。

(as) busy as a bee

shí fēn máng lù
十分忙碌

 例句 ----------------------------

The baker is busy as a bee in the morning.

早上，麵包師傅忙得不可開交。

(as) free as a bird

zì yóu zì zài
自由自在

✦ 例句 ----------------------------

As soon as the summer vacation started,
I felt free as a bird.

暑假一開始，我就感到自由自在了。

(as) stubborn as a mule

fēi cháng gù zhi
非常固執

✨ 例句 --------------------------------

He is stubborn as a mule. He refuses to see a doctor even though he is very ill.

他非常固執。即使他病得很嚴重，仍拒絕求醫。

動物

at a snail's pace

huǎn màn de
緩慢地

 例句 ------------------------------

There is a long queue and the customers are moving at a snail's pace.

很多人在排隊，顧客以緩慢的速度前進。

black sheep

bài lèi
敗類

 例句

He is the black sheep of the family who always causes troubles.

他是家中的敗類，經常惹麻煩。

cry wolf

láng lái le
狼來了

 例句 —— 此慣用語多說明某人屢次說謊。

I do not think he has a stomach ache.
He has cried wolf so many times.

我不認為他肚子痛，他嚇唬我們太多次了。

eat like a horse

shí liàng jí dà
食量極大

 例句 -

I always eat like a horse after swimming.

游泳後,我總是食量極大。

fight like cat and dog

zhēng chǎo bù xiū
爭吵不休

 例句

They fight like cat and dog and never get along at work.

他們爭吵不休,在工作上合作不來。

get one's ducks in a row

zhǔn bèi jiù xù
準備就緒

例句 -------------------------

We have to get our ducks in a row before the conference starts.

會議開始前，我們要把一切事項準備好。

have a bee in one's bonnet

duì mǒu shì rù mí
對（某事）入迷

✨ 例句 ----------------------------

Jack is a coffee lover. He has a bee in his bonnet about it.

傑克是咖啡愛好者，對咖啡很入迷。

have a frog in one's throat

shuō huà kùn nan
說話困難

 例句

She cannot sing today. She has lost her voice and had a frog in her throat.

她今天不能唱歌。她失聲了，說話有困難。

have ants in one's pants

zuò lì bù ān
坐立不安

✨ **例句**

> 此慣用語多由興奮或焦躁的情緒引起。

The kids were very excited about the outing. They had ants in their pants.

孩子們對這次郊遊興奮得<u>坐立不安</u>。

have bigger fish to fry

yǒu gèng zhòng yào de shì yào zuò
有更重要的事要做

 例句 -

I do not have the time to watch TV with you. I have bigger fish to fry.

我沒有時間和你看電視,我有更重要的事要做。

動物

have butterflies in one's stomach

fēi cháng jǐn zhāng
非常緊張

 例句

I had butterflies in my stomach before the performance.

表演開始前,我感到非常緊張。

hold your horses

tíng yī tíng
停一停

 例句

Hold your horses! We do not have enough money for this new tablet.

停一停！我們不夠錢買這部新的平板電腦。

like a bull in a china shop

bèn shǒu bèn jiǎo
笨手笨腳

 例句

She got fired because she was like a bull in a china shop and broke many plates.

她被解僱，因為她笨手笨腳，摔掉了很多碟子。

like a deer caught in the headlights

xià huài le

嚇壞了

 例句 ----------- deer 可換成 rabbit。

He was like a deer caught in the headlights when the car accident happened.

車禍發生時，他嚇壞了。

like a fish out of water

bù zì zai
不自在

 例句 - - - - - - - - 此慣用語多用於陌生環境。

When I first came to this school, I was like a fish out of water.

剛剛上這所學校時，我感到很不自在。

rain cats and dogs

qīng pén dà yǔ
傾盆大雨

 例句

We got stuck in the station because it was raining cats and dogs.

我們困在車站了，因為外面下着傾盆大雨。

separate the sheep from the goats

fēn chū yōu liè
分出優劣

102

 例句 ------ separate 可換成 sort out。

There were many participants. The preliminary round separated the sheep from the goats.

參賽者有很多，預賽把他們分出了優劣。

take to sth like a duck to water

rú yú dé shuǐ
如魚得水

103

 例句 ----------

> 此慣用語多說明天生就會做某事。

Mia took to roller-skating like a duck to water.

美雅天生就會滾軸溜冰。

動物

watch sb like a hawk

yán mì jiān shì
嚴密監視

104

 例句

Shh! Mr Chan is watching us like a hawk.

安靜點!陳老師正在盯着我們。

when pigs fly

jué bù kě néng fā shēng
絕不可能發生

 例句 ----------------------------

He is very lazy. He will do the revision when pigs fly.

他很懶惰。他絕不可能會溫習。

ENG × 粵語

ENG × 普通話

a breath of fresh air

ěr mù yì xīn de rén huò shì
耳目一新的人或事

 例句 -

The new girl is so cheerful that she brings a breath of fresh air to our office.

新來的女職員非常開朗，令辦公室耳目一新。

a cloud hanging over

yōu xīn chōng chōng
憂心忡忡

 例句 -

A cloud has hung over her because her puppy is sick.

她憂心忡忡，因為她的小狗生病了。

add fuel to the fire

huǒ shàng jiā yóu
火上加油

108

 例句 -

He is furious now. Don't talk to him.
It just adds fuel to the fire.

他現在很憤怒。不要跟他說話，這只會
火上加油。

(as) fresh as a daisy

jīng shen bǎo mǎn
精神飽滿

 例句 -

After taking the afternoon nap, she is fresh as a daisy.

睡過午覺後,她精神飽滿。

(as) right as rain

wán quán kāng fù
完全康復

110

 例句 -

After taking the medicine and having a good rest, I am now right as rain.

服過藥，好好休息後，我完全康復了。

(as) solid as a rock

fēi cháng jiān gù
非常堅固

 例句 -

Our friendship is solid as a rock.

我們友誼永固。

avoid sth like the plague

_{jìn liàng huí bì}

盡量迴避

 例句 -

Lily is afraid of animals. She avoids them like the plague.

莉莉害怕動物，會盡量迴避牠們。

be snowed under

<ruby>十<rt>shí</rt></ruby> <ruby>分<rt>fēn</rt></ruby> <ruby>忙<rt>máng</rt></ruby> <ruby>碌<rt>lù</rt></ruby>

十分忙碌

113

 例句 ----------------------------

She is snowed under with housework.

家務令她忙得不可開交。

beat about the bush

zhuǎn wān mò jiǎo
轉彎抹角

 例句

Ⓐ Er…I guess I have left my homework at home.

Ⓑ Don't beat about the bush. You simply forgot to do it.

甲 嗯……我想我把功課遺留在家了。

乙 不要轉彎抹角了，你根本就忘記了做功課。

break the ice

dǎ pò lěng chǎng
打破冷場

 例句

On the first day of school, Miss Wong played a game with us to break the ice.

在開學的第一天，黃老師和我們玩了一個遊戲，打破冷場。

call of nature

shàng xǐ shǒu jiān
上洗手間

例句 -

May I be excused? I need to answer the call of nature.

失陪一下，我要上洗手間。

catch some rays

shài yí huì r tài yáng
曬一會兒太陽

117

 例句 -------------------------------

What a lovely sunny day! Let's catch some rays.

今天天氣很好！我們曬一會兒太陽吧。

come rain or shine

fēng yǔ bù gǎi
風雨不改

118

 例句

Come rain or shine, she volunteers for the animal shelter every Saturday.

她逢星期六都會到動物收容所做義工，風雨不改。

in hot water

xiàn rù má fan
陷入麻煩

 例句 -

The mouse has woken the cat and now it is in hot water.

老鼠弄醒了貓，現在牠陷入麻煩了。

leave sb out in the cold

_{lěng luò}
冷落

120

 例句 ------------------

As he was too shy to talk to people, he got left out in the cold in the party.

他太害羞了，不敢和別人交談，所以在派對被冷落了。

let off steam

shì fàng jīng lì
釋放精力

 例句 ----------------------------

Trampolining is the best way for children to let off steam.

跳彈牀是小朋友釋放精力的最佳方法。

light a fire under sb

lìng   mǒu rén   jiā kuài jìn dù
令（某人）加快進度

✦ 例句

Our shop will open soon. Therefore, we lit a fire under the decorators.

我們的店舖快要開張，所以我們催促裝修工人加快進度。

make hay while the sun shines

wù shī liáng jī
勿失良機

例句

Visitors are coming. Let's make hay while the sun shines and keep the shop open.

旅客來了，我們勿失良機，繼續營業吧。

on cloud nine

lè jí wàng xíng
樂極忘形

124

 例句 -

We were on cloud nine when we won the game.

勝出比賽的一刻，我們樂極忘形。

once in a blue moon

hěn shǎo
很少

 例句

She leads a busy life so she cooks for herself once in a blue moon.

她生活忙碌，很少親自下廚。

play with fire

zì qǔ miè wáng
自取滅亡

 例句 --------------------------------

Stay away from the lion. You are playing with fire.

不要走近獅子，你這樣是在自取滅亡。

rain on sb's parade

săo xìng
掃興

 例句

While we were skipping rope, a prefect rained on our parade and stopped us.

我們跳繩時，風紀叫停我們，掃我們興。

see stars

yūn xuàn
暈眩

128

 例句 ------------------------------

I bumped my head on the glass door and I could see stars.

我把頭撞到玻璃門上，感到一陣暈眩。

spread like wildfire

xùn sù chuán kāi
迅速傳開

例句

She cannot keep a secret. If you tell her one, it will spread like wildfire.

她守不住秘密。如果你把秘密告訴她，秘密會迅速傳開。

steal sb's thunder

qiǎng qù fēng tou
搶去風頭

✨ 例句 - - - - - - - - - - - - - - - - - - -

Amy is overdressed. She has stolen my thunder.

艾美打扮得太隆重了，搶去了我的風頭。

take a rain check

xià cì ba
下次吧

✨ 例句 -----------------------------

Ⓐ Would you like to go to the park with us?

Ⓑ Can I take a rain check? I need to finish my homework first.

甲 你要不要跟我們一起去公園？

乙 下次好嗎？我要先完成功課。

the coast is clear

yǐ wú wēi xiǎn
已無危險

 例句 -

The coast is clear. The boar is gone.

沒有危險了，野豬走了。

the tip of the iceberg

<ruby>冰<rt>bīng</rt>山<rt>shān</rt>一<rt>yī</rt>角<rt>jiǎo</rt></ruby>

冰山一角

 例句 --------------------------------

The litter you can see is just the tip of the iceberg.

你看見的垃圾只是冰山一角。

throw caution to the wind

bú gù hòu guǒ
不顧後果

134

 例句 ----------------------------

He threw caution to the wind and climbed up the tree to pick an apple.

他不顧後果爬上樹摘蘋果。

turn over
a new leaf

gǎi guò zì xīn
改過自新

 例句 -

He used to be a bully, but now he has
turned over a new leaf.

他以前是惡霸，但是他現在改過自新了。

under the weather

shēn tǐ bú shì
身體不適

136

 例句 ----------------------------

I am a bit under the weather. I cannot go swimming today.

我有點不舒服，今天不能去游泳了。

up in the air

réng wèi jué dìng
仍未決定

 例句 --------------------------------

Whether we will keep a dog or a cat as a pet is still up in the air.

我們仍未決定要養狗還是貓當寵物。

all roads lead to Rome

tiáo tiáo dà lù tōng luó mǎ
條條大路通羅馬

 例句

You can improve English in many ways.
All roads lead to Rome.

提升英語水平有很多方法。條條大路通羅馬。

at a crossroads

chǔ yú jǐn yào guān tóu
處於緊要關頭

 例句 -

She is at a crossroads — she has to decide which subject to study.

她處於緊要關頭——她要決定修讀哪一科。

ENG × 粵語
ENG × 普通話

build bridges

cù jìn guān xì
促進關係

 例句

> PTA 是 Parent-Teacher Association 的縮寫。

The PTA is formed to build bridges between parents and the school.

成立家長教師會,是為了促進家長和學校之間的關係。

burn sb's bridges

zì duàn tuì lù
自斷退路

 例句 --------

bridges 可換成 boats。

Stop arguing with your boss, or you will burn your bridges.

不要和老闆爭論了，否則你會自毀前程。

by the way

shùn dài yī tí
順帶一提

142

 例句

We need some drinks. By the way, would you like some bread for breakfast tomorrow?

我們需要買一些飲品。順便問一下，明天早餐你想吃麵包嗎？

cross that bridge when one gets to it

chuán dào qiáo tóu zì rán zhí
船到橋頭自然直

 例句

Ⓐ We don't have the tourist map.
Ⓑ That's okay. We'll cross that bridge when we get to it.

甲 我們沒有旅遊地圖。
乙 不要緊，船到橋頭自然直。

ENG × 粵語
ENG × 普通話

drive sb crazy

lìng rén fā nù
令人發怒

144

✦ 例句 -

Stop messing around! You are driving me crazy!

不要再搞亂了！你快把我逼瘋了！

fall by the wayside

bàn tú ér fèi
半途而廢

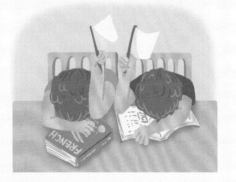

 例句 -

French is too hard that many learners have fallen by the wayside.

法文太難了，很多人半途而廢。

find a way

xiǎng chū bàn fǎ
想出辦法

146

 例句

The farmer found a way to protect the growing crops.

農夫想出了辦法，來保護生長中的農作物。

give the green light to sth

pī   zhǔn
批准

 例句

I wanted to go out with my friends and my mum gave the green light to it.

我想和朋友出去玩，媽媽批准了。

ENG × 粵語

ENG × 普通話

go a long way

qián tú guāng míng
前途光明

 例句 --------

a long way 可換成 far。

He is such a good singer — we believe he will go a long way.

他唱歌很動聽——我們相信他前途一片光明。

go along for the ride

còu rè nao

湊熱鬧

例句

Dad, today is our School Open Day. Shall we go along for the ride?

爸爸，今天是我們學校的開放日，我們要不要去湊熱鬧？

go one's own way

wǒ xíng wǒ sù
我行我素

 例句

While most girls like dresses, she goes her own way and dresses like a boy.

大部分女生喜歡穿裙子,她卻我行我素,穿得像個男生。

go south

biàn chā
變差

 例句 ------------------

Since the supermarket opened, the business of the grocery store has gone south.

自從超級市場開業後，雜貨店的生意就變差了。

go the distance

jiān chí dào zuì hòu
堅持到最後

152

 例句 --------------------------------

Although the athlete twisted his ankle, he insisted on going the distance.

雖然運動員扭傷了腳踝，但是他堅持到最後。

go the extra mile

duō chū yī fēn lì
多出一分力

 例句 -----------------------------

The friendly driver always goes the extra mile for passengers.

這位友善的司機經常為乘客多出一分力。

ENG × 粵語

ENG × 普通話

have a bumpy ride

jīng lì kùn nan
經歷困難

154

 例句 --------------------------

We had a bumpy ride when our business first started.

業務開展初期，我們經歷了很多困難。

hit the road

^{chū} ^{fā}
出發

 例句 -

We are all set. Let's hit the road.

我們準備好了，出發吧。

in the same boat

chǔ jìng xiāng tóng
處境相同

 例句 -

Ⓐ I forgot to bring my lunch. I am starving.
Ⓑ We are in the same boat.

甲 我忘了帶午餐,現在餓極了。

乙 我也是啊。

light at the end of the tunnel

shǔ guāng
曙光

 例句

After a few weeks of treatment, the patient finally saw the light at the end of the tunnel.

經過幾個星期治療,病人終於看見了曙光。

交通

ENG × 粵語

ENG × 普通話

look like the back end of a bus

bù hǎo kàn
不好看

158

 例句 ------------------------------

You have to look like the back end of a bus to play the role of the witch.

如果你飾演巫婆一角，就要裝扮成很醜的樣子。

miles from anywhere

huāng jiāo yě wài
荒郊野外

例句 - - - - - -

anywhere 可換成 nowhere。

Uncle Tim lives miles from anywhere.
It takes us a few hours to get there.

添叔叔住在荒郊野外，我們要花幾小時才到達。

ENG × 粵語

ENG × 普通話

miss the boat

cuò shī shí jī
錯失時機

160

 例句

He wanted to watch the parade but he missed the boat.

他想觀賞巡遊表演，但是他錯失時機了。

on the right track

fāng fǎ dé dàng
方法得當

 例句 --------------------------

Our business is getting better, showing that we are on the right track.

我們的生意越來越好，說明我們的經營方式得當。

on the way to

jí jiāng wán chéng
即將完成

 例句

I am on the way to completing the jigsaw.

我即將完成這幅拼圖了。

paddle one's own canoe

dú lì chǔ shì
獨力處事

 例句 -

When you live alone, you have to paddle your own canoe.

你一個人住時，就要獨力面對所有事情。

plain sailing

shí fēn shùn lì
十分順利

 例句 ------------------------

Our puppy had a surgery. We were relieved that it was plain sailing.

小狗做了手術。手術很順利，我們都鬆了一口氣。

ENG × 粵語   ENG × 普通話

put a brake on

zhì zhǐ
制止

 例句

You have to put a brake on your workout.
Training too hard can cause injuries.

你要減少運動，鍛煉過度可引致受傷。

sail against the wind

bú gù zhòng rén fǎn duì
不顧眾人反對

 例句

The coach sailed against the wind and instructed the members to run in the rain.

教練不顧眾人反對，命令隊員在雨中跑步。

take sb for a ride

qī piàn   mǒu rén
欺騙（某人）

 例句

Ⓐ Sam told me there's a treasure.

Ⓑ He just took you for a ride.

甲 森告訴我這裏有寶藏。

乙 他欺騙你而已。

the end of the road

jìn tóu
盡頭

 例句 -

As the residents moved out, the grocery store reached the end of the road.

隨着居民搬走，這間雜貨店走到盡頭了。

water under the bridge

yǐ chéng guò qù
已成過去

 例句 -

They used to fight a lot but that is all water under the bridge now.

他們以前常常打架，現在一切已成過去。

against the clock

fēn miǎo bì zhēng
分秒必爭

 例句 -

The ambulancemen are working against the clock to save the injured.

救護員正在分秒必爭救助傷者。

all day long

zhěng tiān
整天

例句

He loves his new scooter. He can play with it all day long.

他很喜歡他新的滑板車，可以整天踏着它。

ENG × 粵語　ENG × 普通話

all of a sudden

tū rán
突然

 例句

We were jogging, then all of a sudden a dog popped up and barked at us.

我們正在緩步跑。突然一隻狗跑出來，向我們吠叫。

(as) clear as day

qīng xī yì míng
清晰易明

✨ 例句 ------------------------------

The map is clear as day. You can find the post office easily.

這幅地圖清晰易明，你可以輕易找到郵局。

as soon as

yī
jiù
一⋯⋯就⋯⋯

✦ 例句 ⋯⋯⋯⋯⋯⋯⋯⋯⋯⋯⋯⋯⋯⋯⋯

He turned the TV on as soon as he finished his homework.

他一完成功課，就去開電視。

時間

as time goes by

shí jiān liú shì
時間流逝

175

 例句

As time goes by, the sprout has grown into a tree.

時間流逝，幼苗已長成一棵樹了。

時間

at one's leisure

kòng xián shí
空閒時

176

 例句 ------------------------

You are encouraged to read more books at your leisure.

我們鼓勵你空閒時多閱讀。

better late than never

chí lái zǒng bǐ bù lái hǎo
遲來總比不來好

 例句

Ⓐ Sorry, I am late.
Ⓑ Better late than never.

甲 對不起，我遲到了。

乙 遲來總比不來好。

177

better luck next time

zhù nǐ xià cì hǎo yùn
祝你下次好運

 例句 -

He was only two seconds faster than you. Better luck next time!

他只比你快兩秒。祝你下次好運！

ENG × 粵語 ENG × 普通話

call it a day

dào cǐ wéi zhǐ
到此為止

 例句

此慣用語多用於結束工作時。

We have been working all day long. Let's call it a day.

我們工作了一整天,先到此為止吧。

first come, first served

xiān dào xiān dé
先到先得

180

✨ 例句 -

The free ice cream is first come, first served.

免費雪糕先到先得。

 ice cream的普通話是「冰淇淋」。

in broad daylight

guāng tiān huà rì
光天化日

 例句

Two armed men robbed the bank in broad daylight.

兩名武裝男子在光天化日打劫銀行。

in this day and age

jīn shí jīn rì

今時今日

 例句 ----------------------------

Digital devices are widely used for teaching in this day and age.

今時今日，數碼器材被廣泛應用在教學上。

182

kill time

dǎ fā shí jiān
打發時間

 例句 ----------------------------

He read a few magazines to kill time on the train.

他在火車上看了幾本雜誌來打發時間。

make sb's day

ràng mǒu rén yú kuài
讓（某人）愉快

✦ 例句 ----------------------------

Receiving my grandson's handmade birthday card made my day.

收到孫子親手製作的生日卡，讓我很愉快。

make time

téng chū shí jiān
騰出時間

 例句

In spite of his busy schedule, Marco makes time for running every morning.

即使生活忙碌，馬可每天早上都會騰出時間跑步。

night and day

rì yǐ jì yè
日以繼夜

186

 例句 ----------------------------

The tailor has worked night and day
to make the suit for his client.

裁縫日以繼夜為客人趕製西裝。

not be born yesterday

bú yì shòu piàn
不易受騙

 例句

Ⓐ I was captured by some bad guy, so I am late.

Ⓑ Do you think I will believe that? I was not born yesterday.

甲 我被壞人抓走了，所以我才會遲到。

乙 你以為我會相信？我可沒那麼容易受騙。

once upon a time

hěn jiǔ yǐ qián
很久以前

 例句 - - - - - - -

此慣用語多用於故事開首。

Once upon a time there lived a princess in a castle.

很久以前，城堡裏住着一位公主。

since when...?

hé shí kāi shǐ
何時開始……?

 例句 -

Since when has the living room become a playroom?

客廳何時開始變成了遊戲室?

sooner or later

chí zǎo

遲早

✨ 例句 ------------------------------

🅐 Despite many cover letters sent out, I still haven't got an offer.

🅑 Don't worry. Sooner or later you will get a job.

甲 儘管寄出了很多求職信，但是我還未獲聘請。

乙 不要擔心，你遲早會找到工作。

take your time

màn màn lái

慢慢來

例句

Ⓐ I need a few more minutes to pack my bag.

Ⓑ Take your time.

甲 我需要多幾分鐘收拾行裝。

乙 慢慢來。

the time is ripe

shí jī chéng shú
時機成熟

 例句 ------

I will get you a bicycle when the time is ripe.

時機合適的話，我會給你買一輛雙輪單車。

✏ bicycle的普通話是「自行車」。

the time of one's life

jí yú kuài de shí guāng
極愉快的時光

 例句 ------------------------

The newlyweds had the time of their lives at the wedding.

這對新婚夫婦在婚宴上度過了極愉快的時光。

time flies

shí guāng fēi shì
時光飛逝

194

 例句 -

Time flies! We have known each other
for over 20 years.

時光飛逝！我們認識對方已有20年了。

時間

ENG × 粵語

ENG × 普通話

time hangs heavy

shí jiān guò de hěn màn
時間過得很慢

195

 例句

Time hangs heavy when shopping with mum.

跟媽媽去購物時，時間過得很慢。

a bundle of laughs

yǒu qù de rén huò shì
有趣的人或事

 例句

John is a bundle of laughs so his friends like him very much.

約翰是一個有趣的人，所以他的朋友很喜歡他。

a far cry from

xiāng chà hěn yuǎn
相差很遠

例句 -

City life is a far cry from country life.

城市生活和鄉村生活相差很遠。

actions speak louder than words

xíng dòng shèng yú kōng yán
行動勝於空言

 例句

Ⓐ I wish I could help the old man.
Ⓑ Look! A boy is doing it. Actions speak louder than words.

甲 真希望我能幫助那位老人。

乙 你看，有位男孩正在幫助他。行動勝於空言。

at the top of my voice

shēng sī lì jié
聲嘶力竭

 例句 ----------------------------

When I saw the spider, I screamed at the top of my voice.

看見蜘蛛時，我聲嘶力竭地尖叫起來。

burst out crying

tū rán dà kū
突然大哭

200

 例句 --------------------------------

The girl burst out crying when she saw the vicious dog.

女孩見到惡狗時，突然大哭起來。

easier said than done

zhī yì xíng nán

知易行難

 例句

Ⓐ You should not eat foods which contain sugar, oil and fat.

Ⓑ It is easier said than done.

甲 你不能吃含有糖分、油分和脂肪的食物。

乙 這聽起來很容易，做起來卻很困難。

for a laugh

wèi le qǔ lè
為了取樂

 例句 ----------------------------

He is a stand-up comedian. Many people watch his show for a laugh.

他是獨角喜劇演員，很多人看他的表演都是為了取樂。

give one's word

chéng nuò
承諾

例句 -

Dad gave his word that he would take us to the amusement park tomorrow.

爸爸承諾明天會帶我們去主題公園。

説話

I told you so

wǒ zǎo jiù gào su guò nǐ
我早就告訴過你

204

  例句 ------------------------------

Ⓐ Ouch! It is piping hot!

Ⓑ I told you so.

甲 哎呀！很燙！

乙 我早就告訴過你。

ENG × 粵語　ENG × 普通話

I'll say

dí què shì
的確是

例句

Ⓐ She is a very talented pianist.
Ⓑ I'll say!

甲 她是才華洋溢的鋼琴家。

乙 的確如此！

I wouldn't say no

hǎo de
好的

 例句 ----------

> 此慣用語多用於表示
> 想要某物。

Ⓐ Would you like some cookies?

Ⓑ I wouldn't say no.

甲 要吃一些曲奇餅嗎?

乙 好啊。

if you ask me

wǒ rèn wéi
我認為

 例句

If you ask me, you look much better without make up.

我認為你不化妝時好看得多。

keep one's voice down

jiàng dī shēng liàng
降低聲量

✦ 例句 ----------------------------

Please keep your voice down. Dad is talking on the phone.

請輕聲說話，爸爸正在通電話。

keep one's word

xìn shǒu nuò yán
信守諾言

209

 例句 - - - - - - - - | word 可換成 promise。

He said he would teach me how to swim
and he did keep his word.

他答應過教我游泳，他真的有信守諾言。

ENG × 粵語　ENG × 普通話

lost for words

shuō bù chū huà lái
說不出話來

例句

此慣用語多用於表示震驚或驚訝。

She was lost for words when her colleagues surprised her with the birthday cake.

同事為她準備了生日蛋糕，讓她驚喜得說不出話來。

mum's the word

bǎo shǒu mì mì
保守秘密

 例句 --------------------------------

We are going to throw him a surprise party. Mum's the word!

我們會為他舉辦驚喜派對。你要保守秘密！

only joking

kāi wán xiào ér yǐ
開玩笑而已

 例句 -

This dress is beautiful. I want to try it on — only joking!

這條裙子很漂亮。我想試穿──開玩笑而已！

說話

ENG × 粵語

ENG × 普通話

say cheese

xiào yī gè
笑一個

213

例句 ----------

此慣用語多用於幫別人拍照時。

The photographer said, "Say cheese, children!"

攝影師說:「孩子們,笑一個!」

say goodbye to

shě qì mǒu wù
捨棄（某物）

 例句

If you want to get healthy, you need to say goodbye to junk food.

如果你想身體健康，就要戒掉垃圾食物。

speak of the devil

shuō dào Cáo Cāo　　Cáo Cāo jiù dào
說到曹操，曹操就到

✦ **例句** ----------- speak 可換成 talk。

🇦 We are still waiting for Lily.

🇧 Speak of the devil. Look! She is coming.

甲 我們還在等莉莉。

乙 說到曹操，曹操就到。你看！她來了。

speak one's mind

tǎn yán zhí shuō
坦言直說

✨ 例句 -----

If you do not like this dress, you should speak your mind.

如果你不喜歡這條裙子，就應該坦言直說。

ENG × 粵語　ENG × 普通話

speak for yourself

wǒ bù tóng yì
我不同意

 例句

> 此慣用語多用於對別人的看法表示不同意。

Ⓐ I think the painting is very nice.
Ⓑ Speak for yourself! It looks unfinished.

甲 我覺得這幅油畫很好看。

乙 我不同意,它看上去還未完成。

talk trash

fèi huà lián piān
廢話連篇

 例句

No one wants to talk to him as he always talks trash.

沒有人想跟他說話,因為他經常廢話連篇。

ENG × 粵語　ENG × 普通話

tell me about it

kě bú shì ma
可不是嘛

 例句

> 此慣用語多用於認同別人的說話。

Ⓐ She is so arrogant and rude.
Ⓑ Tell me about it!

甲 她太傲慢無禮了。

乙 可不是嘛!

with one voice

yí zhì de
一致地

 例句

Johnny is helpful. His classmates have chosen him as the monitor with one voice.

莊尼樂於助人。他的同學一致推選他為班長。

word has it

jù shuō

據說

例句

word 可換成 rumour。

Word has it that this supermarket is closing down.

據說這間超級市場即將要倒閉。

a hard nut to crack

jí shǒu de rén huò shì
棘手的人或事

 例句 --------------------------

Mr Chan is fussy. No one wants to deal with this hard nut to crack.

陳先生很挑剔。沒有人想應付這棘手的人。

a piece of cake

qīng ér yì jǔ de shì
輕而易舉的事

 例句 ----------------------------

Turning somersaults is a piece of cake to gymnasts.

對體操運動員來說，翻筋斗是輕而易舉的事。

an apple a day keeps the doctor away

yī rì yī pín guǒ
一日一蘋果，
yī shēng yuǎn lí wǒ
醫生遠離我

 例句

An apple a day keeps the doctor away. Would you like to eat one?

一日一蘋果，醫生遠離我。你要吃一個嗎？

(as) cool as a cucumber

lěng jìng
冷靜

 例句

He is cool as a cucumber despite being trapped in the lift.

雖然他被困在升降機裏，但是他很冷靜。

(as) easy as pie

<small>jí dù róng yì</small>

極度容易

 例句 ----------------------------

Making salad is easy as pie — just toss all the ingredients into a big bowl.

製作沙律極度容易——只需把所有材料放入大碗。

salad的普通話是「沙拉」。

(as) flat as a pancake

shí fēn píng tǎn
十分平坦

 例句 -

This place is flat as a pancake. We can set up our tents here.

這個地方十分平坦，我們可以在這裏紮營。

be like chalk and cheese

jié rán bù tóng
截然不同

228

 例句 -

Although we are twins, we are like chalk and cheese.

雖然我們是雙胞胎,但是我們截然不同。

big cheese

zhòng yào rén wù
重要人物

 例句

He must be a big cheese — even our manager has to seek his advice.

他一定是重要人物——甚至我們的經理都要向他請教。

bread and butter

móu shēng jì néng
謀生技能

230

 例句

Baking is my passion. It is my bread and butter too.

我熱愛烘焙，同時烘焙是我的謀生技能。

bring home the bacon

<ruby>養<rt>yǎng</rt></ruby> <ruby>家<rt>jiā</rt></ruby> <ruby>糊<rt>hú</rt></ruby> <ruby>口<rt>kǒu</rt></ruby>

養家糊口

231

 例句 ----------------------------

He works hard so that he can bring home the bacon.

為了養家糊口，他努力工作。

飲食

butter sb up

_{tǎo hǎo mǒu rén}
討好（某人）

 232

✨ 例句 -----------------------

His clients like him a lot because he always butters them up.

他的客戶很喜歡他，因為他經常討好他們。

飲食

ENG × 粵語

ENG × 普通話

chew the fat

xián tán
閒談

233

 例句 ----------------------------

The girls are sitting in the café and chewing the fat.

女生們在咖啡館坐着閒談。

eat humble pie

rèn cuò
認錯

234

✦ 例句 ------- humble pie 可換成 crow。

He had to eat humble pie because he did not study hard for the exam.

他認錯了，因為他沒有努力溫習預備考試。

飲食

eat like a bird

chī de hěn shǎo
吃得很少

 例句 -

The actress eats like a bird so that she
can keep her figure.

這位女演員吃得很少，以保持苗條體態。

飲食

feast one's eyes on

jìn qíng xīn shǎng
盡情欣賞

 例句

The tourists feast their eyes on the view of the sea.

旅客們盡情欣賞海景。

food for thought

lìng rén shēn sī de shì
令人深思的事

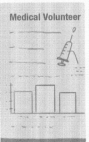

Medical Volunteer

237

例句

Dr Chan has been a medical volunteer for years. His speech gave us food for thought.

陳醫生擔任醫務義工多年，他的講辭值得我們深思。

ENG
×
粵語

ENG
×
普通話

from soup to nuts

cóng tóu dào wěi
從頭到尾

238

 例句

The witness told the police officer about the accident from soup to nuts.

目擊者把意外發生的經過從頭到尾告訴警員。

have a bite to eat

chī xiē dōng xi
吃些東西

239

 例句 --------------------------------

I am hungry. Let me have a bite to eat first.

我肚子很餓，我要先吃些東西。

it's no use crying over spilled milk

yǐ chéng dìng jú　kū yě méi yòng

已成定局，哭也沒用

 例句 ------------------------------

It's no use crying over spilled milk — you should have studied harder.

已成定局，哭也沒用——你早應該努力溫習。

like two peas in a pod

wài biǎo xiāng xiàng
外表相像

例句 --------------------------------

Anna and Belle are twin sisters. They are like two peas in a pod.

安娜和貝兒是雙胞胎姊妹，她們長得很相像。

ENG × 粵語 ENG × 普通話

not one's cup of tea

bù hé xīn yì
不合心意

例句 -

Action film is not my cup of tea. Let's watch a comedy.

動作電影非我所好。我們看喜劇吧。

飲食

ENG × 粵語

ENG × 普通話

packed like sardines

shí fēn jǐ pò
十分擠迫

例句 --------------------------------

The passengers are packed like sardines on the bus.

在巴士上，乘客緊緊擠在一起。

bus 的普通話是「公共汽車」。

ENG × 粵語

ENG × 普通話

pie in the sky

nán yǐ shí xiàn de shì
難以實現的事

 例句 - - - - - - - - - -

此慣用語亦作 castle in the air。

Teaching the kitten to walk on two legs seems to be pie in the sky.

教小貓用雙腳走路，看似是難以實現的事。

sell like hot cakes

chàng xiāo
暢銷

 例句 --------------------------

The comic is selling like hot cakes.

這本漫畫很暢銷。

spill the beans

xiè lòu mì mì
洩露秘密

 例句 -

He spilled the beans about your plan to break out of prison.

他洩露了你的逃獄計劃。

246

take it with a pinch of salt

bù néng jìn xìn
不能盡信

 例句

pinch 可換成 grain。

Ⓐ The ad says the product can help people grow tall in three days.

Ⓑ You'd better take it with a pinch of salt.

甲 廣告說這個產品能讓人在三天內長高。

乙 你最好不要盡信。

飲食

ENG × 粵語   ENG × 普通話

the apple of one's eyes

zhǎng shàng míng zhū
掌上明珠

248

 例句 -

My grandma loves me very much. She says I am the apple of her eyes.

祖母很疼愛我。她說我是她的掌上明珠。

the best thing since sliced bread

jí hǎo de shì wù
極好的事物

 例句 -

My new watch is multifunctional. It is the best thing since sliced bread.

我的新手錶有很多功能，是極好的產品。

飲食

the bitter fruits of

è guǒ
惡果

250

✨ **例句**

He is tasting the bitter fruits of not studying hard.

他正在承受不努力學習的惡果。

the cream of the crop

jīng yīng
精英

 例句 ----------------------------

The students who participated in the quiz competition are the cream of the crop.

參加問答比賽的學生都是精英。

the icing on the cake

jǐn shàng tiān huā
錦上添花

 例句

I enjoy dancing on stage. Winning an award is the icing on the cake.

我享受在台上跳舞，能夠獲獎更是錦上添花。

walk on eggshells

xiǎo xin yì yì
小心翼翼

 例句 -

My supervisor is touchy. We have to walk on eggshells around her.

我的上司容易發怒，我們在她身邊要小心翼翼。

ENG × 粵語

ENG × 普通話

a dime of dozen

suí chù kě jiàn
隨處可見

 例句 --------------------------

Tropical fruits are a dime of dozen in our country.

在我們的國家，熱帶水果隨處可見。

a stone's throw

hěn duǎn de jù lí
很短的距離

 例句 -------------------------

🅐 How can I get to the nearest convenience store?

🅑 It is only a stone's throw away. Just go straight ahead.

🇨 請問最近的便利店在哪裏？

🇿 距離這裏很近。你一直向前走吧。

anything but

yī diǎn yě bù
一點也不

✦ **例句** ----------

此慣用語多用於強調
語氣，表示否定。

This story book is anything but interesting.
這本故事書一點也不有趣。

as a last resort

zài pò bù dé yǐ shí
在迫不得已時

 例句 -

If we cannot get out of here, we will call 999 for help as a last resort.

如果我們找不到出路，迫不得已時會打999求助。

(as) bright as a button

shí fēn cōng míng
十分聰明

 例句

He is bright as a button. He has got all the questions solved.

他十分聰明，答對了所有問題。

(as) clean as a whistle

shí fēn gān jìng
十分乾淨

 例句 ----------------------------

After the spring-cleaning, the house is clean as a whistle.

大掃除過後，家裏變得十分乾淨。

(as) fit as a fiddle

shí fēn jiàn kāng
十分健康

260

 例句

Although my grandfather has reached the age of 80, he is fit as a fiddle.

雖然祖父80歲了，但是他仍很健壯。

(as) light as a feather

<ruby>輕<rt>qīng</rt></ruby> <ruby>如<rt>rú</rt></ruby> <ruby>羽<rt>yǔ</rt></ruby> <ruby>毛<rt>máo</rt></ruby>

 例句 -

This folding umbrella is light as a feather.
Let's buy it.

這把摺疊傘輕如羽毛，就買它吧。

(as) pretty as a picture

piào liang rú huá
漂亮如畫

262

 例句 ----------------------------

Look at the sunset on the beach. It is pretty as a picture.

看看沙灘上的日落，漂亮如畫。

物件

(as) regular as clockwork

shí fēn zhǔn shí
十分準時

 例句

Grandpa watches the news at 7 a.m. every morning, regular as clockwork.

祖父每天早上七時都會看新聞，十分準時。

物件

 ENG × 粵語

 ENG × 普通話

(as) smooth as silk

róu huá rú sī
柔滑如絲

264

 例句 -

I like my doll. Its hair is smooth as silk.

我很喜歡我的洋娃娃。它的頭髮柔滑如絲。

(as) thin as a rake

shí fēn shòu xuē
十分瘦削

 例句 -

You are thin as a rake. You need to eat more.

你太瘦削了，要多吃一點東西。

(as) tough as old boots

shí fēn jiān qiáng
十分堅強

 例句 ----------

> 此慣用語也可形容食物難以咀嚼。

She was tough as old boots. She did not cry even though she was seriously injured.

她十分堅強。即使她受重傷,也沒有哭。

at the drop of a hat

háo bù yóu yù
毫不猶豫

 例句 -

If I had enough money, I would buy this car at the drop of a hat.

如果我有足夠金錢，我會毫不猶豫買下這輛車。

物件

at the end of one's tether

<ruby>筋<rt>jīn</rt></ruby><ruby>疲<rt>pí</rt></ruby><ruby>力<rt>lì</rt></ruby><ruby>竭<rt>jié</rt></ruby>

 例句 -

After spending the whole day with kids, I am at the end of my tether.

和小朋友們相處了一整天，我筋疲力竭了。

a chip off the old block

hé fù mǔ xiāng sì
和父母相似

 例句

此慣用語多指樣貌、神態、性格等。

Matthew loves football as much as his dad does. He is a chip off the old block.

馬修如同他爸爸一樣熱愛足球，他真像他爸爸。

down to the wire

zhí dào zuì hòu yī kè
直到最後一刻

 例句 --------------------------------

The match was so exciting that it went down to the wire.

這場比賽很刺激，直到最後一刻才分出勝負。

go back to the drawing board

chóng xīn kāi shǐ
重新開始

271

例句 -

The client does not like our design so we have to go back to the drawing board.

客戶不喜歡我們的設計，我們要重新構想。

in the middle of something

zhèng máng zhe
正忙着

 例句

I will call you back. I am in the middle of something.

我稍後回撥電話給你，我正忙着。

judge a book by its cover

yǐ mào qǔ rén
以貌取人

例句 --------------------------------

He runs very fast. You cannot judge a book by its cover.

他跑得很快，你不能以貌取人。

物件

just the thing

zhèng xū yào de dōng xi
正需要的東西

274

 例句

After an exhausting day of work, a good rest is just the thing for dad.

經過一天疲憊的工作，爸爸正需要的是好好休息。

ENG × 粵語

ENG × 普通話

look for a needle in a haystack

dà hǎi lāo zhēn
大海撈針

 例句

Finding your passport at the airport is like looking for a needle in a haystack.

要在機場找回你的護照，就像大海撈針一樣。

made of money

fù yǒu
富有

 例句 ------------------------

The man is made of money. He owns
several properties.

這位男士很富有。他擁有幾個物業。

物件

on the ball

jī líng
機靈

例句 -

Susan is on the ball. She knows how to deal with difficult customers.

蘇珊很機靈。她懂得如何應對麻煩的客人。

on the fence

yóu yù bù jué
猶豫不決

 例句

- -

Bobby is still on the fence about donating blood.

波比還在猶豫是否捐血。

pass the buck

tuī xiè zé rèn
推卸責任

例句

It is your turn to clean the classroom today. Don't pass the buck to me.

今天輪到你清潔教室。不要把責任推卸給我。

物件

sleep like a log

shú shuì
熟睡

 例句 -

Don't worry. He is sleeping like a log.

不用擔心,他很熟睡。

280

stick to sb like glue

nián zhe mǒu rén

黏着（某人）

 例句 -------------------------------

The puppy always sticks to its owner like glue.

小狗總是黏着牠的主人。

sure thing

dāng rán kě yǐ
當然可以

 例句 -

Ⓐ May I try the soup?
Ⓑ Sure thing!

甲 我可以嘗嘗湯嗎？

乙 當然可以！

the ball is in one's court

lún dào　　mǒu rén　　jué dìng
輪到（某人）決定

 例句 -------------------------------

Everything is ready for you to learn to swim. The ball is in your court now.

學游泳的一切所需已準備好了，要不要學就由你來決定。

throw in the towel

rèn shū
認輸

 例句 -

You are so good at chess. I think I have to throw in the towel.

你棋藝高超，看來我只好認輸。

tie the knot

jié hūn

結婚

 例句 ------------------------

After dating for a few years, they finally decided to tie the knot.

他們約會了幾年，終於決定要結婚。

動作

add insult to injury

luò jǐng xià shí
落井下石

286

 例句

You should have helped him up instead of laughing at him. You are adding insult to injury.

你應該扶起他，而不是取笑他。你這樣是在落井下石。

be barking up the wrong tree

zhǎo cuò yuán yīn
找錯原因

例句

此慣用語亦指「用錯方法」。

Mary thought Sam dirtied her doll, but she was barking up the wrong tree.

瑪莉以為森弄污了她的洋娃娃,但是她怪錯人了。

bite one's lip

yì zhì biǎo dá qíng gǎn
抑制表達情感

288

 例句

Everyone bit their lips when they heard someone fart.

聽到有人放屁時，大家都忍着不笑。

bite the bullet

yìng zhe tóu pí
硬着頭皮

 例句

Dad is not at home. Mum has to bite the bullet and scare the mouse away.

爸爸不在家，媽媽只好硬着頭皮嚇退老鼠。

blow sb's mind

令（某人）興奮激動

 例句

The music show was superb. It really blew the audience's mind.

這場音樂表演很精彩，令觀眾驚喜萬分。

come again?

zài shuō yī biàn hǎo ma
再說一遍好嗎？

✦ 例句 ------------------------------

Come again? I couldn't hear you.

再說一遍好嗎？我聽不清楚你說什麼。

come first

jū yú shǒu wèi
居於首位

 例句

此慣用語多用於說明最重要的人或事。

Safety should always come first.

安全永遠最重要。

cut corners

tān tú fāng biàn
貪圖方便

 例句

Peter cut corners on his homework by filling out answers randomly.

彼得做功課時**貪圖方便**，隨意填上答案。

動作

cut sb some slack

wǎng kāi yī miàn
網開一面

 294

 例句 -

The manager cut him some slack because
he is a trainee.

經理對他網開一面，因為他是實習生。

動作

 ENG × 粵語 ENG × 普通話

drop the ball

fàn cuò
犯錯

 例句 -

The worker dropped the ball when he forgot to bring the tools.

這名工人犯錯了，忘記了帶工具。

動作

easy does it

xiǎo xīn diǎn
小心點

 例句 - - - - - -　此慣用語多用於提醒別人。

Easy does it! The box is heavy.

小心點！箱子很重。

give it a rest

bú yào zài shuō le
不要再說了

 例句 ------------------------------

Give it a rest! You have been grumbling all morning.

不要再說了，你已經抱怨了整個早上。

動作

give it a shot

^{shì yī shì}
試一試

298

 例句 ----------------------------

This game looks fun. Let's give it a shot.

這個遊戲看起來很有趣，我們試一試吧。

give sb a piece of one's mind

_{zé} _{bèi}
責備

 例句

They were so noisy. I gave them a piece of my mind.

他們太嘈吵了，我教訓了他們一頓。

動作

go one better

gèng shèng yī chóu
更勝一籌

300

✨ 例句

Canned juice tastes good but fresh squeezed juice goes one better.

罐裝果汁很好喝，但是鮮榨果汁更勝一籌。

動作

go too far

zuò de tài guò fèn
做得太過分

 例句 --------------------------------

You should not have pranked your friend.
You went too far.

你不應該捉弄朋友。你做得太過分了。

hang in there

jiān chí zhù
堅持住

 例句 ----------------------------

Hang in there! I am coming to save you.

堅持住，我來救你。

hit the books

nǔ lì wēn xí
努力溫習

 例句 ------------------------

I must hit the books now, or I will fail the exam.

我必須努力溫習，否則考試會不及格。

hit the sack

shàng chuáng shuì jiào
上牀睡覺

 例句 - - - - - - - - - - - - 　　sack 可換成 hay。

He has to get up early tomorrow so he has already hit the sack.

他明天要早起牀，所以他已經上牀睡覺了。

動作

it takes two to tango

shuāng fāng dōu yǒu zé rèn
雙方都有責任

305

例句

It takes two to tango. If you had not provoked him, he wouldn't have been mean to you.

你們雙方都有責任。如果你不激怒他,他就不會對你刻薄。

動作

kick the bucket

sǐ diào
死掉

 例句

Be careful! Don't fall in the river, or you will kick the bucket.

小心點！不要掉進河裏，否則你會沒命。

ENG × 粵語

ENG × 普通話

let's face it

shí huà shí shuō
實話實說

 例句 -

Let's face it. We are hopeless to win against them.

實話實說吧，我們贏不了他們的。

動作

make a name for oneself

chéng míng
成名

 例句 ------------------------------

Julie has made a name for herself as a science fiction writer.

茱莉以科幻小說作家成名。

play dirty

shuǎ huā zhāo
耍花招

✨ 例句 -

Don't play with him. He always plays dirty by pushing others over.

不要跟他玩。他常常耍花招，推倒別人。

play safe

jǐn shèn qǐ jiàn
謹慎起見

310

 例句

- -

I do not want to miss the flight. To play safe, I will arrive at the airport earlier.

我不想錯過航班。謹慎起見，我會早些到達機場。

pull oneself together

zhěng dùn qíng xù
整頓情緒

 例句 ----------------------------

After the quarrel, they pulled themselves together and apologised to each other.

爭吵過後,他們整頓情緒,向對方道歉。

pull out all the stops

jié jìn suǒ néng
竭盡所能

✨ 例句 -------------------------------

The firemen pulled out all the stops to save the victims.

消防員竭盡所能拯救災民。

put the finishing touches to

zuò zuì hòu rùn shì
作最後潤飾

 例句 ----------------------------

Grandma is putting the finishing touches to the scarf.

祖母正在為圍巾作最後潤飾。

roll one's sleeves up

zhǔn bèi kāi shǐ gōng zuò
準備開始工作

314

例句

Everybody, roll your sleeves up and start setting up the game booth.

各位，請準備開始布置遊戲攤位。

send sth flying

shuāi dǎo　　mǒu wù
摔倒（某物）

 例句 -----------------------

The waiter slipped on the floor and sent the plates flying.

侍應生滑倒了，碟子摔倒在地。

can't help

rěn bu zhù

忍不住

316

例句 -

The kitten is so cute. I can't help touching it.

小貓很可愛，我忍不住摸牠。

can't wait

jí bù jí dài
急不及待

 例句 --------------------------------

I got a present from my uncle. I can't wait to open it.

叔叔送了一份禮物給我。我急不及待要打開它。

couldn't agree more

<ruby>完<rt>wán</rt></ruby> <ruby>全<rt>quán</rt></ruby> <ruby>同<rt>tóng</rt></ruby> <ruby>意<rt>yì</rt></ruby>
完全同意

 例句

Ⓐ We should turn off our phones now.
Ⓑ I couldn't agree more.

甲 我們現在應該關掉電話。

乙 我完全同意。

ENG × 粵語   ENG × 普通話

don't mention it

bú yào kè qi
不要客氣

 例句

Ⓐ Thank you for the lift.
Ⓑ Don't mention it!

甲 謝謝你載我一程。
乙 不要客氣！

don't you dare
nǐ dǎn gǎn
你膽敢

320

 例句 - - - - - - - -

> don't you dare 多用於
> 警告對方不要做某事。

Ⓐ I will tear up your picture.
Ⓑ Don't you dare!

甲 我要撕掉你的圖畫！

乙 你膽敢！

in no mood

méi yǒu xīn qíng
沒有心情

 例句 -

I am sorry. I am in no mood to play with you.

不好意思。我沒有心情跟你玩。

last but not least

zuì hòu dàn tóng yàng zhòng yào
最後但同樣重要

 例句

You should prepare food, water and a bed for your puppy. Last but not least, you should give it love.

你要為小狗準備食物、水和牀。最後但同樣重要，你要給牠愛心。

neither here nor there

wú guān zhòng yào
無關重要

 例句

Ⓐ Would you like to play football or basketball?

Ⓑ It is neither here nor there. We cannot go out because it is raining.

甲 你想踢足球還是打籃球？

乙 都不重要了。外面正在下雨，我們不能外出。

never mind

bú yào jǐn
不要緊

 例句 --------------------------

Ⓐ I am sorry. I missed the ball.
Ⓑ Never mind, we still have a chance of winning.

甲 對不起,我錯失了一球。

乙 不要緊,我們還有機會贏的。

否定

no biggie

méi shén me dà bù liǎo

沒什麼大不了

325

 例句 - - - - - - - -

biggie 可換成 big deal。

Ⓐ Mum, I am sorry. I made a mess.
Ⓑ No biggie! Let's clean it up together.

甲 媽媽，對不起，我弄得一團糟。

乙 沒什麼大不了！我們一起清理吧。

no kidding

shuō zhēn de
說真的

326

 例句

No kidding, this vase is worth more than 10,000 dollars.

說真的，這個花瓶價值過萬元。

no longer

bú zài

不再

 例句

Dad used to drink a lot of coffee but he no longer drinks that much.

爸爸以前喝很多咖啡，但是他現在不再喝那麼多了。

no matter how

wú lùn
無論

 例句 ----------

no matter 也可搭配 what 和 why。

No matter how tired he is, he still spends time playing with his children.

無論他有多疲倦，他仍會花時間和孩子玩樂。

no problem

méi wèn tí

沒問題

 例句

> 此慣用語多用於回應別人的請求，亦指「不要客氣」。

Ⓐ Can you help me take a photo, please?
Ⓑ No problem.

甲 請問可以幫我拍照嗎？

乙 沒問題。

no way

bù
不

✦ 例句

> 此慣用語多用於拒絕他人。

🅐 Mum, can I buy the robot?
🅑 No way! You have too many robots.

甲 媽媽，我可以買這個機械人嗎？
乙 不！你已經有很多機械人了。

✏️ robot 的普通話是「機器人」。

no wonder

nán guài
難怪

331

 例句 -

The department store is having a sale.
No wonder there is a long queue.

百貨公司正在進行促銷，難怪有這麼多人
排隊。

none of sb's business

<ruby>與<rt>yǔ</rt></ruby>（<ruby>某<rt>mǒu</rt></ruby><ruby>人<rt>rén</rt></ruby>）<ruby>無<rt>wú</rt></ruby><ruby>關<rt>guān</rt></ruby>

與（某人）無關

 例句

Ⓐ Your drawing is terrible.

Ⓑ It's none of your business. Give it back to me.

甲 你的畫很醜。

乙 這與你無關，把畫還給我。

not enough room to swing a cat

<ruby>空<rt>kōng</rt></ruby> <ruby>間<rt>jiān</rt></ruby> <ruby>狹<rt>xiá</rt></ruby> <ruby>小<rt>xiǎo</rt></ruby>

kōng jiān xiá xiǎo
空間狹小

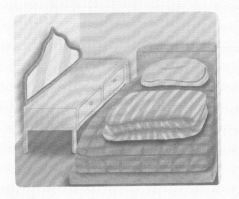

 例句

This dressing table is too big. There is not enough room to swing a cat.

這張梳妝枱太大了，使空間很狹小。

not up to much

<ruby>質<rt>zhì</rt>素<rt>sù</rt>不<rt>bù</rt>好<rt>hǎo</rt></ruby>

 例句 -

The products of that shop are not up to much.

那間商店的產品質素不好。

not bear thinking about

bù gǎn xiǎng xiàng
不敢想像

例句

Ⓐ What would happen if the rope broke?
Ⓑ It doesn't bear thinking about.

甲 如果繩子斷了，會發生甚麼事？
乙 簡直不敢想像。

not have a clue

méi yǒu tóu xù

沒有頭緒

336

 例句 - - - - -

此慣用語亦作 have no clue。

Ⓐ Who stole a bite of my cake?

Ⓑ I don't have a clue.

甲 是誰偷吃了我的蛋糕？

乙 我沒有頭緒。

not know whether to laugh or cry

kū xiào bù dé
哭笑不得

 例句 -------------------------------

When my girl put on my make-up, I did not know whether to laugh or cry.

女兒用我的化妝品時,我哭笑不得。

not on speaking terms

hù bù lǐ cǎi
互不理睬

✦ 例句 ----------------------------

Mum feels bad to see that her daughters are not on speaking terms.

媽媽看見女兒們互不理睬，感到很難過。

not rocket science

bìng bù tè bié kùn nan
並不特別困難

339

✦ 例句

Ⓐ It is difficult to assemble this bookshelf.
Ⓑ Let me see. It's not rocket science.

㊒ 這個書櫃很難組裝。
㊜ 讓我看看。這並不是特別困難。

not the end of the world

bù shì tài zāo gāo
不是太糟糕

340

 例句

I know you feel bad about losing the game but it is not the end of the world.

我知道輸掉比賽讓你很難過，但是不至於糟糕得像世界末日。

not to worry

bié dān xīn
別擔心

✨ 例句 ----------------------------

Ⓐ Oh no! We are too late.
Ⓑ Not to worry. We can take the next bus.

甲 糟糕！我們太遲了。

乙 別擔心，我們可以坐下一班巴士。

 bus 的普通話是「公共汽車」。

a blessing in disguise

yīn huò dé fú
因禍得福

 例句 ----------------------------

We missed the bus, but it seems to be a blessing in disguise.

雖然我們趕不上巴士，但是看來因禍得福了。

✎ bus 的普通話是「公共汽車」。

around the corner

jiù zài fù jìn
就在附近

 例句 -

The toilets are just around the corner.

洗手間就在附近。

as long as

zhǐ yào
只要

 例句 -

As long as you are tall enough, you can ride the roller coaster.

只要你夠高，就可以坐過山車。

as you wish

xī suí zūn biàn
悉隨尊便

 例句

wish 可換成 please。

Ⓐ I would like a drink.
Ⓑ Sure. As you wish.

甲 我想要一杯飲品。
乙 好的,悉隨尊便。

at sixes and sevens

luàn qī bā zāo

亂七八糟

 例句 -

When mum is not at home, everything is at sixes and sevens.

媽媽不在家時,一切都變得亂七八糟。

at this rate

zhè yàng xià qù
這樣下去

 例句

At this rate, we will definitely lose the game.

這樣下去，我們必敗無疑。

better safe than sorry

<ruby>有<rt>yǒu</rt></ruby> <ruby>備<rt>bèi</rt></ruby> <ruby>無<rt>wú</rt></ruby> <ruby>患<rt>huàn</rt></ruby>

有備無患

 例句

Bring along an umbrella. Better safe than sorry.

帶上雨傘吧,有備無患。

come out of one's shell

bú zài wèi suō
不再畏縮

 例句 ----------------------------

Hailey has come out of her shell since she went to kindergarten.

自從上了幼稚園，海莉就不再畏縮了。

dying for sth

jí kě wàng
極渴望

 例句 ------------------------------

She is my favourite writer. I am dying for a book signed by her.

她是我最喜愛的作家。我極渴望得到她親筆簽名的圖書。

fair enough

hǎo ba
好吧

 例句 - - - - - - - - - - - - - - - - - -

Ⓐ I need to go to the tutorial class so I cannot tidy up with you.

Ⓑ Fair enough.

甲 我要去上補習班，所以我不能跟你收拾了。

乙 好吧。

feel like a new man

gǎn jué hǎo hěn duō
感覺好很多

✨ 例句 ----------- man 可換成 woman。

I feel like a new man after taking a shower.
洗完澡後，我感覺好很多。

get the feeling of sth

kāi shǐ zhǎng wò
開始掌握

 例句 -----------------

After trying for an hour, I started to get the feeling of how to ride a bike.

經過一小時的嘗試，我開始掌握到如何騎單車了。

✏️ bike的普通話是「自行車」。

good for you

tài hǎo le
太好了

此慣用語多用於祝賀
別人成功。

🅐 I got into my dream university!
🅑 Good for you!
甲 我考進了心儀的大學！
乙 太好了！

good idea

hǎo zhǔ yi
好主意

 例句 ------------------------

Ⓐ Shall we play chess?
Ⓑ Good idea!

甲 我們下棋好嗎？

乙 好主意！

good luck

zhù hǎo yùn
祝好運

 例句 -

"Good luck!" the coach said to the team before the game.

比賽開始前，教練向隊員說：「祝你們好運。」

had better

<small>zuì hǎo zhè yàng zuò</small>

最好這樣做

 例句

> 此慣用語多用於給予建議，
> had 多以縮寫表達。

We are going to walk a lot. You'd better change a pair of comfortable shoes.

我們要走很多路，你最好換一雙舒服的鞋。

have a quick temper

róng yì fā nù
容易發怒

 例句 ------------------------------

He has a quick temper. He yells at his subordinates for minor problems.

他很容易發怒，會因小問題而怒罵下屬。

其他

 ENG × 粵語

 ENG × 普通話

here you are

gěi nǐ de
給你的

 例句 ------

此慣用語多用於把東西交給別人，are 可換成 go。

Ⓐ Can I use your ruler?
Ⓑ Here you are.

甲 我可以用你的直尺嗎？

乙 給你的。

359

how about...?

zěn me yàng
……怎麼樣？

 例句 --------

此慣用語多用於提出建議。

Ⓐ What would you like to eat for dinner?
Ⓑ How about ordering in a pizza?

甲 你今晚想吃什麼？
乙 叫外賣吃薄餅怎麼樣？

how come?

zěn me huì
怎麼會……?

 例句 -

Ⓐ How come you are so late?
Ⓑ There was a car accident.

㊫ 你怎麼會這麼遲?

㊜ 剛才出了交通意外。

keep sb posted

通知（某人）

最新情況

 例句

Ⓐ After taking the medicine, I feel much better now.

Ⓑ Great! Take more rest. Keep me posted.

甲 吃藥後，我現在好多了。

乙 那就好了！多休息，隨時告訴我最新情況。

make yourself at home

qǐng zì biàn
請自便

✨ 例句 ----------

> 此慣用語是在家招呼客人時的禮貌用語。

Welcome — make yourself at home.

歡迎進來，請自便。

more than

fēi cháng
非常

 例句 -----------------------------

Ⓐ Do we have enough food for the picnic?
Ⓑ Don't worry. We have more than enough.

甲 我們有足夠的食物去野餐嗎？

乙 不用擔心，我們的食物綽綽有餘。

ENG × 粵語　ENG × 普通話

oh my God

wǒ de tiān a
我的天啊

 例句

> 此慣用語多用於表示驚奇、憤怒或震驚。

Ⓐ We fell into a mud puddle.

Ⓑ Oh my God!

甲 我們掉進了泥坑。

乙 我的天啊！

on it

zhèng zài chǔ lǐ
正在處理

 例句 -

Don't panic! I'm on it!
別驚慌！我正在處理！

one by one

yī gè jiē yī gè
一個接一個

 例句 ----------------------------

The students entered the hall one by one.

學生一個接一個進入禮堂。

one of a kind

dú yī wú èr

獨一無二

368

 例句 -

The sculpture is made of marble and metal. It is one of a kind.

這個雕像用大理石和金屬製成，獨一無二。

out of this world

jí hǎo de
極好的

 例句 -

Grandma, your apple pie is out of this world!

祖母，你做的蘋果餡餅美味極了！

pleased to meet you

hěn gāo xìng rèn shi nǐ
很高興認識你

 例句

此慣用語多用於初次見面時。

Ⓐ This is my wife.
Ⓑ Pleased to meet you.

甲 這位是我太太。

乙 很高興認識你。

practice makes perfect

shú néng shēng qiǎo
熟能生巧

例句

You will get better at football if you keep working on it. Practice makes perfect.

如果你繼續努力，你的足球球技就會進步，熟能生巧。

same here

_{wǒ yě shì}

我也是

 例句 -

Ⓐ I am still at the office.
Ⓑ Same here.

甲 我還在辦公室。
乙 我也是。

sb's pride and joy

mǒu rén de
（某人的）

kuài lè hé jiāo ào
快樂和驕傲

 例句 --------------------------------

Sarah is bright and loving. She is her parents' pride and joy.

莎拉又聰明又有愛心，是父母的快樂和驕傲。

see you later

zài *jiàn*
再見

 例句 -

Ⓐ I have to go now.
Ⓑ See you later.

甲 我要走了。
乙 再見。

sort of

yǒu diǎn r
有點兒

375

 例句 -

He is sort of rude. When people say hello to him, he just looks at them.

他有點兒無禮。人們向他打招呼時,他只看着他們。

sure enough

(guǒ rán)
果然

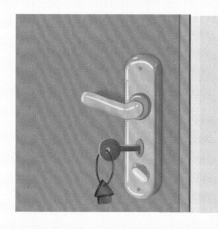

 例句

She said she had lost the key, and sure enough, it is still in the door.

她說她不見了鑰匙,果然,鑰匙還插在門上。

take care

bǎo zhòng
保重

✨ 例句 - - - - - - - - 此慣用語多用於道別時。

Ⓐ Goodbye!
Ⓑ Bye, take care!

甲 再見！
乙 再見，保重！

take it easy

fàng sòng diǎn
放鬆點

 例句 -

Take it easy. We still have a lot of time.

放鬆點。我們還有很多時間。

thank goodness

xiè tiān xiè dì
謝天謝地

 例句

goodness 可換成 God 和 heaven。

Thank goodness you caught the vase!

謝天謝地,你把花瓶接住了!

the luck of the draw

quán píng yùn qì
全憑運氣

380

 例句 ------------------------

If the wind is strong enough, the kite will go higher — it depends on the luck of the draw.

如果風力夠強，風箏會飛得更高──這全憑運氣。

the name of the game

zuì zhòng yào de tè zhì
最重要的特質

例句 ----------------------------

To be a good teacher, patience is the name of the game.

要成為好老師,最重要的特質是耐性。

the whole nine yards

yīng yǒu jìn yǒu
應有盡有

 例句 -

We have prepared everything for our unborn baby — a cot, a pushchair, a baby carrier — the whole nine yards.

我們已為胎兒準備了一切東西：嬰兒牀、嬰兒車、背帶……應有盡有。

think twice

shēn sī shú lù
深思熟慮

 例句

twice 可換成 long and hard。

The weather is getting worse. Think twice about going out for a walk.

天氣轉差了。你想清楚是不是要外出散步吧。

through thick and thin

zài rèn hé qíng kuàng xià
在任何情況下

384

 例句 -

My parents always stand by me through thick and thin.

在任何情況下，父母總是會支持我。

too bad

tài kě xī le
太可惜了

 例句 - - - - - - - -

> 此慣用語多用於對事情表達婉惜。

Ⓐ I failed my test.
Ⓑ That's too bad.

甲 我測驗不及格。

乙 太可惜了。

新雅兒童英文圖解字典

慣用語 Idioms

作　　者：Elaine Tin
繪　　圖：Pikki Ng
責任編輯：黃稔茵
美術設計：劉麗萍
出　　版：新雅文化事業有限公司
　　　　　香港英皇道499號北角工業大廈18樓
　　　　　電話：（852）2138 7998
　　　　　傳真：（852）2597 4003
　　　　　網址：http://www.sunya.com.hk
　　　　　電郵：marketing@sunya.com.hk
發　　行：香港聯合書刊物流有限公司
　　　　　香港荃灣德士古道220-248號荃灣工業中心16樓
　　　　　電話：（852）2150 2100
　　　　　傳真：（852）2407 3062
　　　　　電郵：info@suplogistics.com.hk
印　　刷：中華商務彩色印刷有限公司
　　　　　香港新界大埔汀麗路36號
版　　次：二〇二四年一月初版

ISBN: 978-962-08-8223-4
©2024 Sun Ya Publications (HK) Ltd.
18/F, North Point Industrial Building, 499 King's Road, Hong Kong
Published in Hong Kong SAR, China
Printed in China

作者簡介

Elaine Tin 田依莉

持有翻譯及傳譯榮譽文學士學位和語文學碩士學位，曾任兒童圖書翻譯及編輯。熱愛英文教學，喜與兒童互動，故於二零一四年成為英文導師，把知識、經驗和興趣結合起來，讓學生愉快地學習。她認為每個孩子都是獨特的，如能在身旁陪伴和輔助，就能激發他們的興趣和潛質。著有英文學習書《LEARN and USE English in Context 活學活用英文詞彙大圖典》及《中英成語有文化 IDIOMS AND PHRASES》。後者榮獲第三屆香港出版雙年獎「語文學習組別最佳出版獎」。

繪者簡介

Pikki Ng

設計系畢業，目前是個自由插畫師及設計師，曾於各類型出版社擔任設計師多年。在學時期開始插畫創作，喜歡畫胖胖的動物和食物。經常花很多時間在思考，觀察事情，聽人們説話。